I'm Reading About

NEW JERSEY

The Garden State!

GALLOPADE

by Carole Marsh

Printed and Manufactured in Peachtree City, GA., USA
www.gallopade.com

Book design: John Hanson

Editorial manager: Janice Baker

New Jersey is a great state.

It is one of a kind.

What makes New Jersey special?

Let's read about it and see!

NATIVE AMERICANS

Who lived in New Jersey first?

Native Americans did!

They moved around to find food.
They hunted in New Jersey's woods.
They fished in New Jersey's rivers.
They gathered fruits and seeds and nuts.

EXPLORERS

The first explorers came to New Jersey in 1524.
They came from the country of Italy.

Giovanni da Verrazzano was their leader.
He and his men were looking for new land!

SETTLEMENT

A group of Dutch men came to America.
They started the first settlement in New Jersey.
They named it Bergen.

New Jersey was one of the original 13 colonies.

Bergen
Bergen

STATEHOOD

New Jersey was the third state
to join the United States of America!

Isn't it great,
to be a state!
I bet New Jersey
could hardly wait!

New Jersey became a state in 1787.

New Jersey
The 3rd State
Here we are!

FLAG

I am the state flag.
I was adopted in 1896.

What color am I?
I am "buff." Buff is yellowish-beige.

Look at me.
What else do you see?

I fly high over the state of New Jersey!

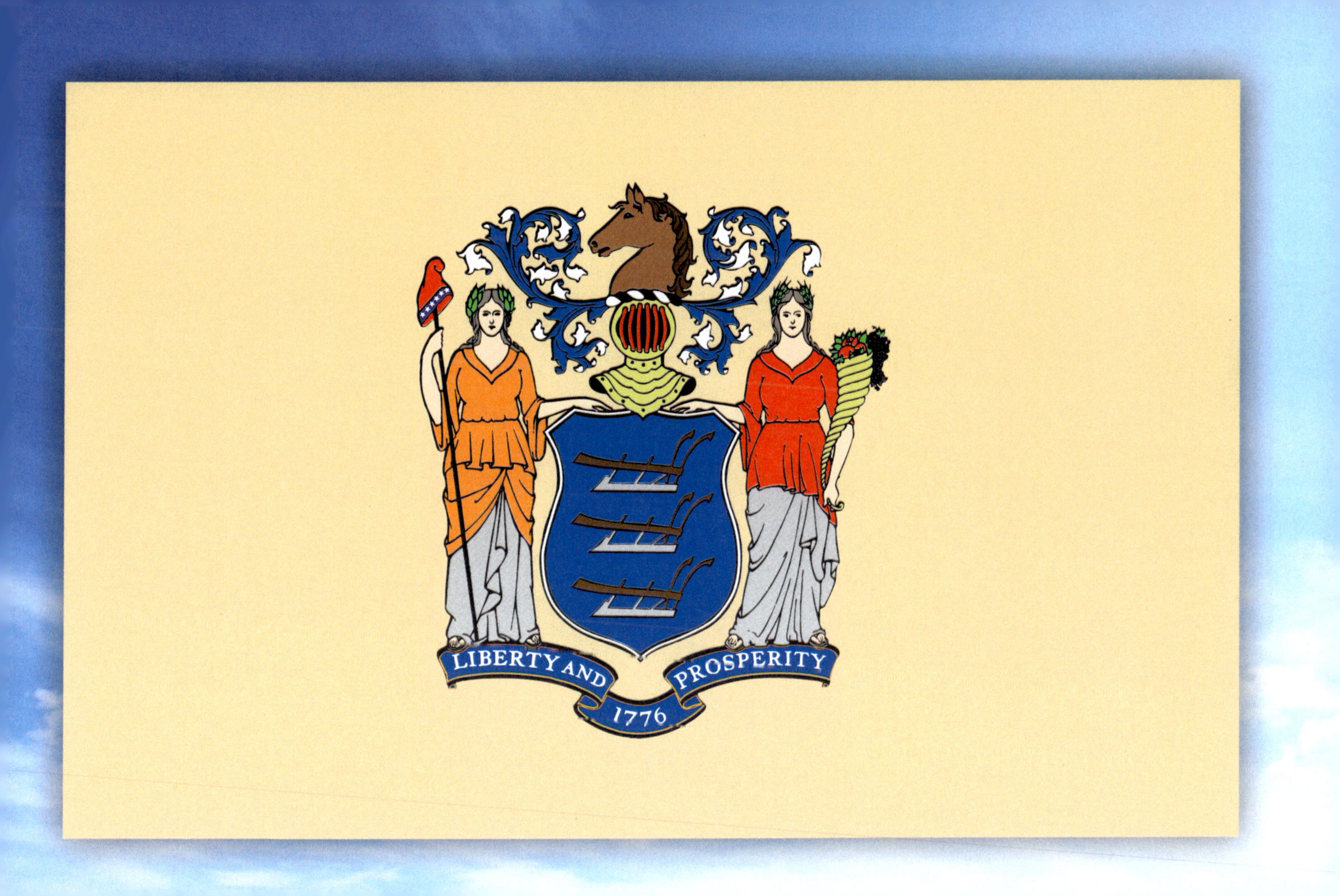
LIBERTY AND
PROSPERITY
1776

CAPITAL

Say hello to Trenton,
the capital city of New Jersey!

There is an important building in Trenton.
It is the State House.
New Jersey's laws are made there!

State House

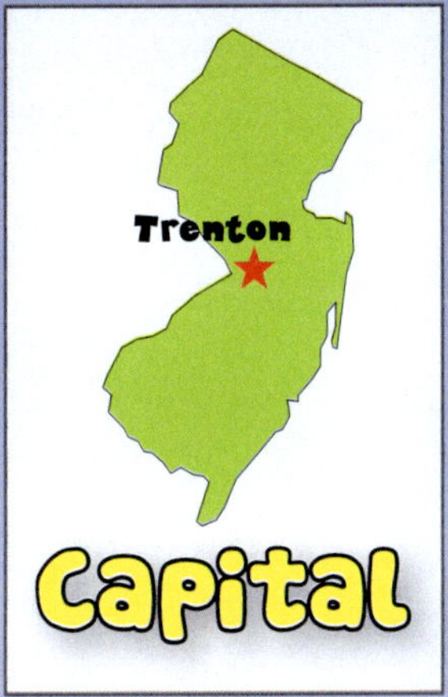

SEAL

I am a seal,
but I am not the State Seal.
If I were, I would be very important.
I would be stamped on many official papers.
(Ouch, that might hurt!)

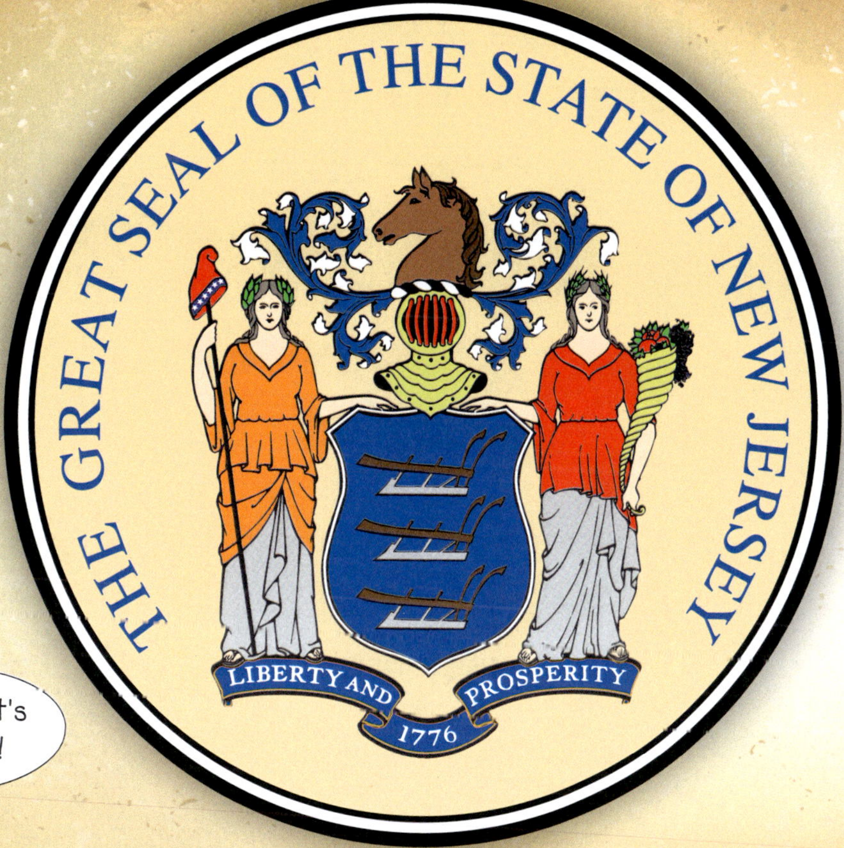
THE GREAT SEAL OF THE STATE OF NEW JERSEY
LIBERTY AND PROSPERITY
1776

Now, that's official!

NICKNAME

State nicknames are fun!
State nicknames are great!
They share fun facts
about each state!

New Jersey's nickname is "The Garden State."

New Jersey has about 10,000 farms!

The Garden State

BORDERS

Look at New Jersey.
New Jersey is in a region called "the Northeast."

New Jersey borders three other states.
Find them on the map!

New Jersey was named after a British island named Jersey.

Borders

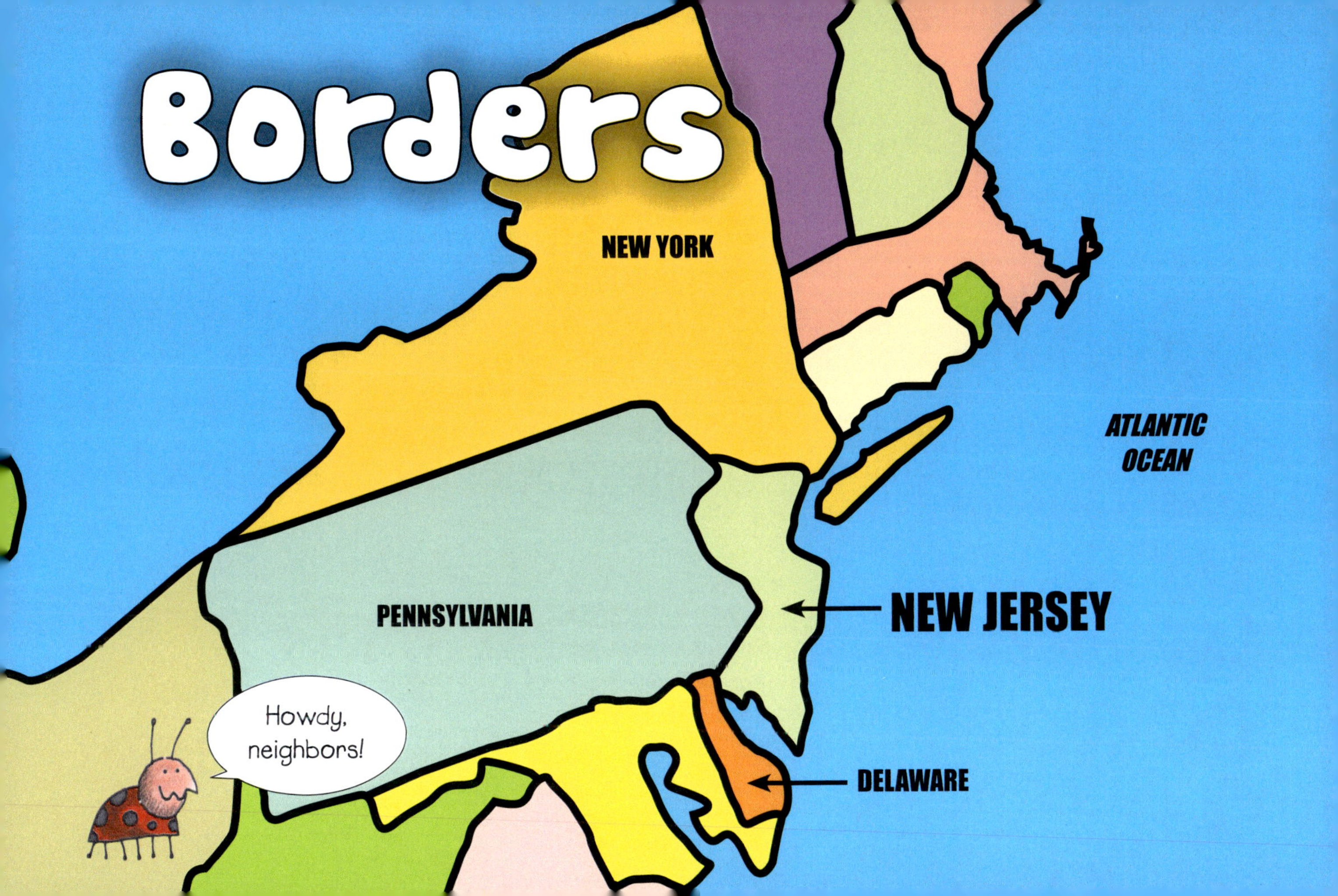
NEW YORK
ATLANTIC
OCEAN
PENNSYLVANIA
NEW JERSEY
DELAWARE
Howdy,
neighbors!

PRESIDENTS

The President is the leader of our country.
He lives in Washington, D.C.
That is the capital of the United States.

The President lives in a big house called the White House.

Two United States Presidents are from New Jersey!

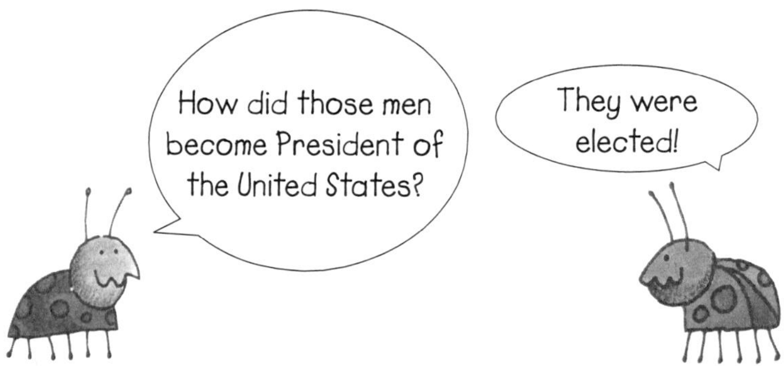

Grover Cleveland
22nd and 24th President
Woodrow Wilson
28th President

Many famous people

Zebulon Pike

Explorer who discovered Pike's Peak in Colorado

Alice Paul

Feminist who worked to gain women the right to vote

Edwin "Buzz" Aldrin

Astronaut who was the second person to walk on the moon

call our state home!

Let's hang out!

Dave Thomas
Founder of Wendy's hamburger restaurant chain

Antonin Scalia
Associate Justice of the U.S. Supreme Court

Christine Todd Whitman
First female governor of New Jersey

Eastern Goldfinch

BIRD

I am the state bird, and I fly
over New Jersey, proud and high.

As I fly, up in the sky,
I flap my wings to tell you "Hi!"

The New Jersey state bird is the Eastern Goldfinch.

Common Meadow Violet

FLOWER

I am the Common Meadow Violet.
I am the state flower.

I grow where it's warm and sunny.
I bloom in spring and summer.
I help make New Jersey beautiful!

Look at me! Smell me!
My blooms are used to make
candies and jellies!

Red Oak

TREE

I am a Red Oak—I'm the state tree.
All over New Jersey is where to find me.

My roots run deep, they keep me strong.
I can live for hundreds of years—that's very long.

I stand up straight, big and tall.
Don't climb too high—it would hurt to fall!

Honeybee

I am the Honeybee.
I am the state insect.

I might sting you if you bother me,
But really, I am your friend.

I carry pollen from flower to flower.
I make honey.
I help New Jersey crops grow.

BZZZZZZZZZZ!

INSECT

Atlantic Ocean
Surf's up!

BEACHES

Let's go to the beach!

We can swim in the waves.
We can play in the sand.

We can build a big castle
where water meets land.

New Jersey's beaches are home to many animals:

Sea Turtles **Fish** **Birds** **Crabs** **Dolphins** **and More!**

Lakes

We can wade in the water.
We can ride on a boat.

We can jump off the dock
onto an inner tube float!

Lake Hopatcong is the largest
lake in New Jersey.

LAKES

Salt Marsh

SALT MARSH

The salt marsh is a flooded area between the ocean and the land.
There are many acres of salt marsh along the coast of New Jersey!

This habitat is home to many animals:

Crabs Snails Mussels Birds Shrimp and More!

The salt marsh floods several times a day!

Atlantic City

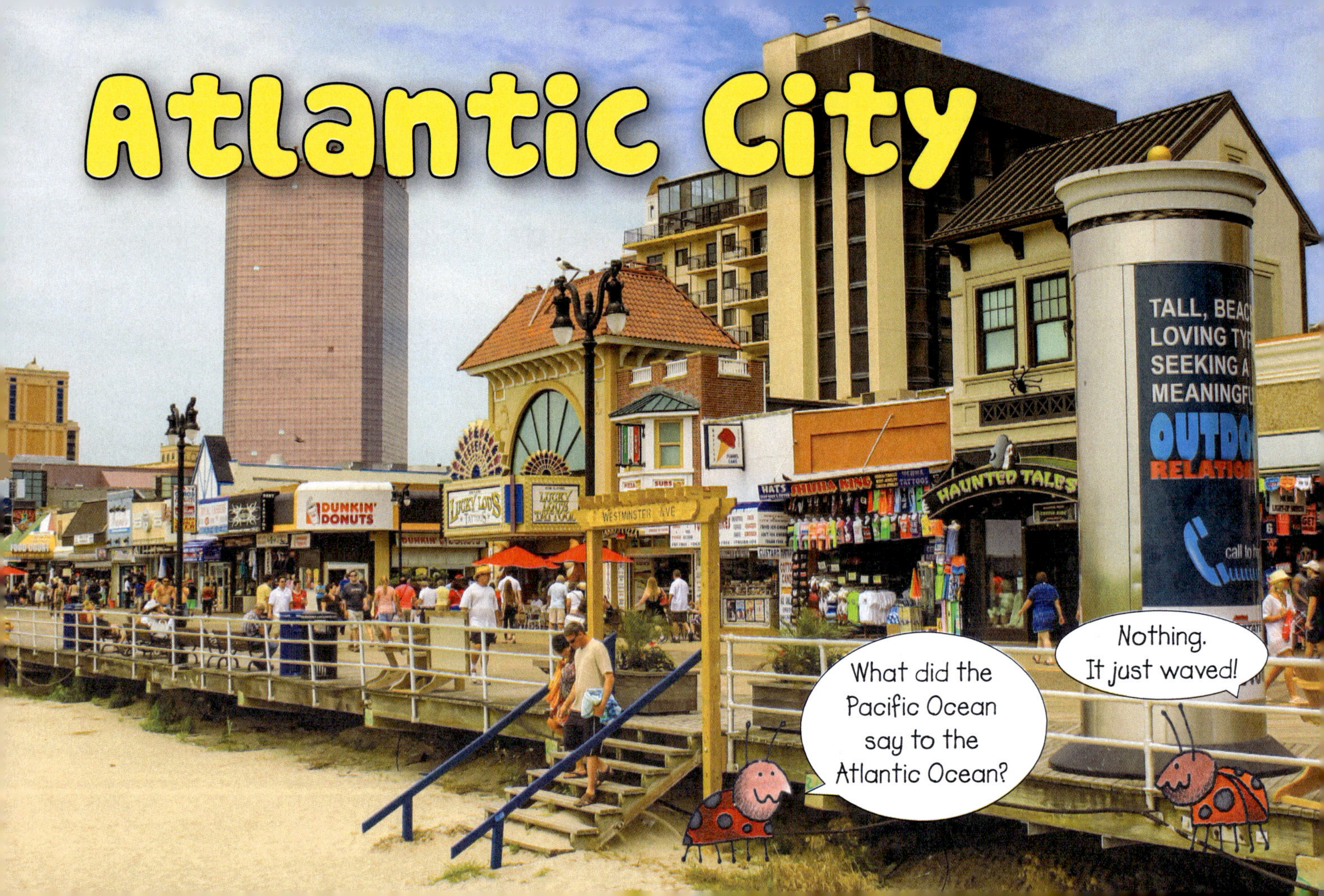

LANDMARK

Atlantic City is a beach town in New Jersey.
It is known for its boardwalks.
The first boardwalk was built to keep sand out of hotel lobbies!
Many visitors vacation in Atlantic City each year.

Atlantic City inspired the board game *Monopoly*.
The property names are actual places in Atlantic City!

New Jersey Crops

AGRICULTURE

New Jersey has many farms.
Why?
Because New Jersey has good soil and a mild climate!

Some of the top crops grown in New Jersey are:

Cranberries **Blueberries** **Corn** **Soybeans**

Sports in New Jersey

SPORTS

Baseball! Basketball! Football! Hockey!
New Jersey has it all.

Whether you like to watch or play,
You are sure to have a ball!

Devils **Thunder** **Tigers**

Scarlet Knights

Pirates

& More!

New Jersey: Home of Thomas Edison and His Inventions

CLAIM TO FAME

Thomas Edison was an amazing inventor!
He worked in a laboratory in Menlo Park, New Jersey.
He invented more than 1,000 items!

Thomas Edison's inventions include:

- phonograph
- motion picture camera
- long-lasting electric light bulb

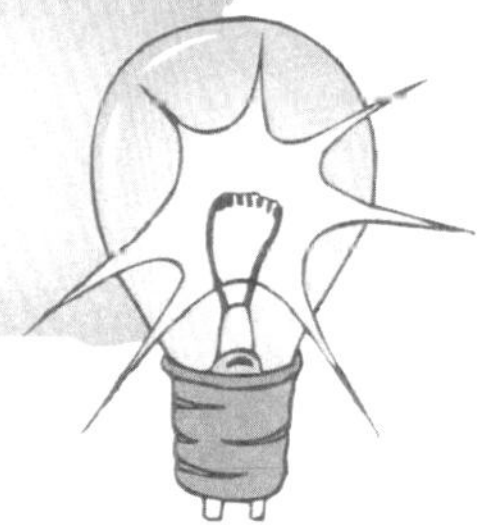

GLOSSARY

astronaut: a person who travels to space

boardwalk: a wooden walkway along a beach or waterfront

climate: weather conditions in an area over a long period of time

colony: a settlement ruled by another country

feminist: a person who supports equal rights for women

habitat: a place where plants or animals naturally live

laboratory: a room or building where scientific experiments take place

laws: rules made by the government

pollen: a yellow powder that helps plants make new plants